I0671088

Jadella Lies

Sonja Howard

Text and illustrations Copyright © 2015 Sonja Howard.

Cover Design by Sonsational Creations with thanks to Jessica, Kirstine and Caitlin.

This book is a work of fiction from the author's imagination, any resemblance to people or incidents is coincidental.

1ˢᵗ Edition, 2015.

All rights reserved.

Cataloguing-in-publication data available from the National Library of Australia.

ISBN: 978-0-646-93877-6

Mission Beach, Queensland, Australia.

Itchy Emu Press

All rights reserved. No part of this book may be reproduced in any form or by any electronic or mechanical means, including information storage and retrieval systems, without permission in writing from the publisher, except by a reviewer who may quote brief passages in a review. Please send enquiries to sonsationalcreations@outlook.com.

DEDICATION

To all those who believed in me.

And all those who dare to dream.

CONTENTS

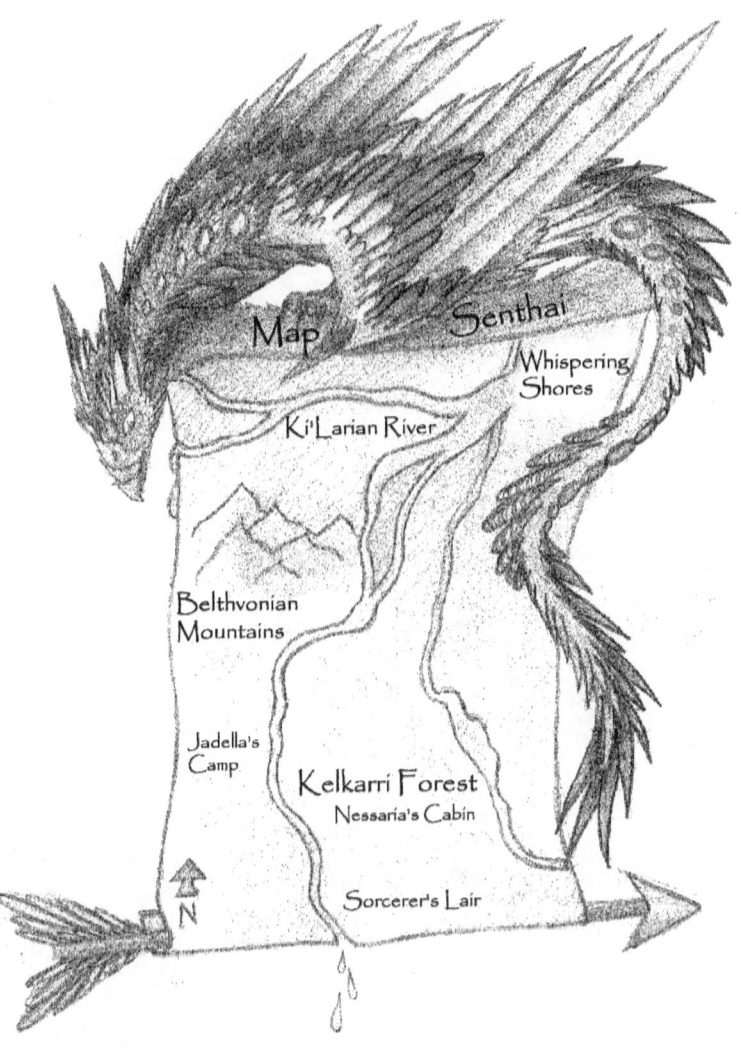

Map

Senthai

Whispering
Shores

Ki'Larian River

Belthvonian
Mountains

Jadella's
Camp

Kelkarri Forest

Nessaria's Cabin

Sorcerer's Lair

N

Chapter 1

the lone figure

Moonlight drifted through the trees overhead. Twigs cracked and smacked together as wind whistled through them, tearing at their leaves like greedy thieves. Clouds haunted the sky, swallowing what light they could as they made their way across the blackening highway. Shadows stalked through the brush, ducking behind trees as a lone figure neared them with a dreaded lantern.

When had she come to think of everything as though it was intent on doing some wrong? The cloaked figure shook her head. The wind had never hurt her, nor the clouds or shadows. When had she become so untrusting? Mind you, it was hardly surprising given her circumstances.

She let her fingers drift to her side, ensuring her purse was still strapped tightly to her belt. Yes, there it was. Safe… for now. She walked on. It had been a long walk made even lengthier by the winding track she had taken. She could not risk being followed. She had to hide, she had to be safe.

Her feet dragged a little as she entered the clearing. Although shrouded in shadows, a few objects could be made out – a desk, some scattered bones and sheets hanging from trees. It was a hovel of some sort; hardly the sort of place the figure had expected the Sorcerer to dwell.

'Name yourself!' The voice, thick with glamour and rage, boomed out from the darkness. Light grew steadily around the clearing, chasing the shadows from its presence. At the centre of the glow stood a woman, tall with wavy dark hair and a scowl that could stop a dragon in its tracks. The Sorcerer leant on a crooked staff, though the figure had a feeling it was far more than a walking aid.

'My name is not important,' replied the figure, 'I seek the Sorcerer that resides in this place; I need her help.'

The Sorcerer stepped forward, spreading her arms arrogantly. 'Then speak to me your request. I don't have all day.'

Swallowing her growing dread, the figure replied 'I need a sleeping potion. One that can be reversed by no simple means. One from which I- My victim, cannot be awoken.'

The Sorcerer smiled wickedly, 'And who, may I ask, is your victim?'

'Someone more dangerous than you can ever imagine.'

'Yet you wish only to make them sleep? How... Weak.' The Sorcerer scoffed, twirling her staff between her fingers.

'Will you do it?'

The Sorcerer paused, slowly looking back at her. Her eyes were hard, face emotionless. Then suddenly she grinned – somehow this was worse. 'Yes, I shall do as you ask; your victim shall sleep for all eternity.'

2

Grinning wickedly, the Sorcerer spun on her heels, quickly searching her messy desk. After several excruciating seconds - during which time the Sorcerer had knocked over almost every jar, pot and skull - a vial rolled out from behind a spell book.

'Ah... Would you like me to come back later?'

The Sorcerer snatched up the vial victoriously, holding it to the light. 'Banish the thought.' She bowed extravagantly, reaching her hand out towards the figure, vial in palm, 'enjoy your safety.' The figure went to take it, but the vial was snatched away, 'and my payment?'

Nodding, the figure reached inside her cloak. Her fingers, numb with the cool morning air, fumbled around her purse. After a moment she found the string, detached it from her belt and handed it to the Sorcerer, who snatched it greedily, examining the contents with a smirk.

'I take it that is sufficient?'

Flapping her hands, the Sorcerer glanced up, 'Yes yes, fare thee well etcetera etcetera.' She handed her the vial and turned away.

'Thank you, you have done the world a great favour.' The figure grasped the potion with both hands, taking a deep breath. Then she turned and walked away, careful to take an even more complex path than on her way there.

She did not see the Sorcerer watch her leave. She did not hear her utter beneath her breath, 'Indeed I have, for now the world will be safe. A sleeping potion? Pfft. Whoever heard of such folly. Death is the only true form of rest.

 Chapter 2

the mercenary with no name

The Mercenary with No Name - infamous warrior, sword fighting extraordinaire, most deadly, murderous fiend known to man – leant back against a tree and smiled. This was it, it was finally going to happen. The Mercenary let one hand drop to her sword, and pulled her cloak over her face with the other. She was a walking shadow of doom. She was death personified. She was… CRACK!

The tree upon which she lent snapped suddenly, the rotten bark splintering around her as she stumbled backwards. *Damn it. So much for stealth.* She shook the woodchips from her clothes and stood, biting her lip in frustration. Through the trees she could see her target turn, tremble a little, then bolt into the undergrowth. With a groan, the Mercenary followed, looping around at a sufficient distance to remain unseen and unheard. With any luck, her target would assume it was a griffin making a particularly ungraceful landing.

The Mercenary continued to follow the cloaked figure for a good hour – she seemed determined to take the most complicated and impractical path possible through the rainforest. Smart, but not smart enough. Eventually she stopped on the bank of a river. For a moment she looked around, then quickly darted back into the undergrowth. Slowly the Mercenary snuck forward, ducking behind a tree. Through the bushes she could see the figure enter a small camp, defined only by the loosely hanging fabric walls that must have provided some protection from the elements. What a pathetic home for someone so powerful. Finally, she was in the Mercenary's grasp. Slowly drawing her sword, the Mercenary stepped forward.

Her target, of course, was the Great Jadella of Legend; a woman more powerful than any creature in all the worlds. A woman who, supposedly, had the ability to control the hearts and minds of everyone on Senthai. A woman too cowardly to ever use them. Very few had ever seen Jadella, but the Mercenary had managed to track down a centaur who, after a little violent persuasion, was willing to direct her to the woman's last rumoured location. It had not been easy, but now the Mercenary had her. Jadella's powers were about be hers forever.

'My lady? Back so soon?' Another woman, shorter than the first, looked up from within a small hovel.

'Yes.' replied Jadella, pulling her hood back. A cascade of brown hair spilled around her shoulders. She was the epitome of beauty; standing drenched in sunlight, her snake-bite piercings glinting in the morning glow. The Mercenary was taken aback for a moment. It seemed reasonable that such a powerful woman would be so beautiful, but it was odd to see her. She had heard stories of the Great Jadella since she was a child; now she had a face to go with the name.

'And you have it?' continued the short one, probably Jadella's hand-maiden.

'Yes, I have it.'

'You're really going to do this aren't you?'

'Yes.'

The Mercenary snuck closer.

'Please, my lady. There has to be another way.' Pausing, the Mercenary tilted her head. This was curious. What were they talking about? She ducked behind a tree and listened.

'It is the only way.' Jadella replied shortly.

The maid continued to plead, 'We can ask your family, they will surely take you back in. They can protect you.'

'My family may be rich, but they are not powerful. I ran for a reason, and due to some blessing you chose to follow me. You are my one true friend.'

'But-'

'You know as well as I that my family crave my powers just as much as those who hunt me.' Jadella snapped, 'I cannot go on living as a prisoner of my own power.'

'Please my lady.'

Enough was enough. The Mercenary stood and walked towards the two figures, still careful to keep quiet. Somehow they did not seem to notice her, or if they did, they did not care.

Resting a hand on her maid's shoulder, Jadella continued, 'When all this drama has calmed, go to the Sorcerer. She will have the cure. But until then you must swear to leave me sleeping. I cannot be extorted when I'm asleep. Swear to me.'

The maid looked at the ground hesitantly, then back up at Jadella, 'I swear.'

Suddenly it became clear. Jadella was poisoning herself. The Mercenary rushed forward, determined to stop her. Something stopped her. It was like slamming face-first into a wall. But there was no wall. The Mercenary threw herself against the invisible barrier futilely. She could not reach the women. She could not even get close. Her prize was going to be ripped away from her, and there was nothing she could do about it.

Jadella took a sip of the potion. The Mercenary's hear sank. She smashed at the invisible wall with her fist, but it did no good. Jadella cringed, apparently still unaware of her attempted saviour, she took another sip. Within seconds the vial was finished, but to the Mercenary it felt like a lifetime. She waited for Jadella to keel over.

'Um...'the two women sat awkwardly for several moments.

'Perhaps it didn't work?' Jadella's maid suggested, barely keeping the relief from her voice. Then Jadella's eyes rolled back in head and she fell to the ground. The magical barrier fell with her. Kneeling by her mistress's side, the Maid tried to make her comfortable. 'Sleep well, my lady. I will wake you when the time is right. When no more people hunt your power   you   shall   again   be   free.'

Able at last, the Mercenary with No Name stalked forward, 'Well this is interesting.'

The maid jumped, fumbling around for something to defend herself with, but remained by Jadella's side, 'Who are you? How long have you been there?'

7

'Long enough.' Slowly the Mercenary circled the maid, her anger at having been denied her prize – at least for now – battled with the thrill of the coming kill.

Visibly quaking, the maid stood. 'Then you know it's too late. You cannot get to her or her powers now.'

'True. But I could not have come in any sooner. That wretch had a magical barrier over this place. Really quite inconvenient.'

Backing away, the maid smiled slightly. She was still positioned between the Mercenary and Jadella, but there was no chance she could win in a fight. She lowered her head and whispered something.

'What was that?' the Mercenary snapped.

The maid glanced up, 'Nothing. You've failed. Leave now and you may live to see another dawn.'

'Oh such big talk from such a little girl.' The Mercenary chuckled, 'But I heard it with my own ears. There is a cure.'

'But you will never find it. I won't tell you anything!'

With lightning speed, the Mercenary shoved the maid. She fell to the ground, dirt spraying around her. Slowly, steadily, the Mercenary drew her sword. 'You don't need to. All I need is your identity.'

Glaring up at her, the maid spat, 'Why? Is yours so despicable you can't bare it any longer? You, who threatens an innocent woman. Who are you?'

'Guess.'

The maid stared at the sword. Her eyes widened, 'Oh god. You're him aren't you. The Mercenary with No Name.'

Scowling, the Mercenary yanked back her hood. 'I too am a woman you fool!' she snarled. Why does everyone assume she is a man? 'And I do have a name, not that any of you commoners shall ever hear it. But I'm sure yours is a pretty name, how 'bout I take it?' Without further delay, the Mercenary plunged the blade downwards. Blood spewed around the black steel, staining the ground around them.

'Great. This was meant to be a nice easy 'take over the world' sort of gig.' The Mercenary sheathed the blade and turned back to Jadella, snatching up the vial. She looked so peaceful, which only enraged the Mercenary further. 'Now I have to see a Sorcerer, and god knows how that'll complicate things!'

Shaking her head, she stomped away. There was a Sorcerer not far from here; Jadella would be safe until she got back. The powerful woman was smart enough to hide her lodgings. It was pure luck that had led the Mercenary to her. Slipping the cloak back over her head, the Mercenary with No Name disappeared into the shadows.

Chapter 3

the cure

The Sorcerer raised her arms high, basking in the glory of her magical powers. The woman before her, dressed drably in a brown, mud-stained cloak, bowed her head respectfully. Smiling, the Sorcerer prepared her greatest act yet, summoning fire to burst from the shadows in a flurry that would block the morning sky from view-

'Please ma'am, my mistress is in dire need of your help. There is no time.' the woman interrupted.

The Sorcerer faltered. This was not right. No one interrupted her. 'Is that so?' she said rigidly, curling her fingers around her staff. She would have to save the fire trick for another time.

'Yes oh great and powerful Sorcerer.' This was more like it, 'My mistress, she is the great Jadella of legend - she who has the power to bring peace to this land. A great illness has befallen her, one which you supplied the means there-to. She was poisoned by a potion contained within this bottle.' The woman held up a small vial. The same vial she, the Sorcerer had given to that other figure early that morning.

With a scream, the Sorcerer snatched the vial and tossed it to the ground, 'That fool! I gave that stupid woman this

10

potion. It must have been her. Oh I will hunt her down that slithering-'

'No, m'lady.' The servant interrupted again. 'Jadella poisoned herself. She took it to save herself from those who hunted her.'

'Who? Who hunted her?'

'The Mercenary with No Name. But he is dead, I killed him myself Jadella must now be awoken. Please.'

Again the Sorcerer faltered, 'You killed him?' she blurted.

'Yes ma'am. Please, there is no time. You must give me the cure.' The servant paused, 'You do have it don't you?'

The Sorcerer glared at her for a long moment. When she spoke again, her voice was calm. 'There is a cure, though it is not in my possession.'

Again the servant's persona cracked, 'Then where is it?'

Stepping forward, the Sorcerer allowed her head to tilt enigmatically to the side, 'Not yet. You see, there is this one thing I can't quite get my head around. Why would Jadella put herself into a deep sleep to protect against a man so easily killed by a simple maid. Surely such extreme measures would be the result of a far greater threat. Unless...' She flicked her wrist, pointing at the 'maid'.

The 'maid' frowned, confused, and opened her mouth to speak. She did not get the chance. On cue, a demonic creature raced from the shadows and launched at her. The 'maid' went down like a tonne of bricks, pinned beneath the snarling monster; it was a skinny humanoid creature with a hairy face and very large teeth which it held close to the throat of its captive. The Sorcerer had raised Windera from a cub, clothed it and taught it to understand various languages. It was loyal to her alone. Smiling, the Sorcerer stepped closer to the duo.

'Let me go, you insolent scum, or I'll gut you like a freaking-'

'Is that so?' the Sorcerer chuckled, leaning down to smile in the face of her captive. She had figured it out. She knew exactly who this imposter was. 'You know I expected more from such an infamous warrior. Then again I also thought you were a man. Surprises really do come in pairs.'

The Mercenary with No Name struggled, almost throwing the creature from her back, 'Oh yeah? Call off your ghoul and I'll give you a real demonstration.'

Again the Sorcerer laughed, 'Why on Senthai would I do that? It would be far more amusing to watch you torn limb from limb. Don't you agree?' She turned to leave. As amusing as it would be to see her little minion Windera feast, she had more important matters to attend to.

'So you don't want Jadella's power then?'

'But of course. Hence why I'm killing you. I have three days before the poison reaches her pretty little heart. Plenty of time to bring her back.' Part of her thought it odd that Jadella had willingly taken the potion – which she must have known would do more than make her sleep – but she ignored the thought. Jadella was probably under a lot of pressure. Or, perhaps, it was some sort of suicide attempt. Either way, the Great Jadella of legend was now her plaything, and she had a lot work to do.

'So you know where she is then?'

The Sorcerer turned around slowly, 'What?'

'That's right. She's hidden, cloaking spell around her and everything. You'll never find her.' The Mercenary replied, doing her best to look tough beneath the salivating Windera. She failed. Dismally.

'What are you saying?'

'I'm saying you need me. I followed her; I know where she's hidden. Besides, three days? If this potion is as complicated as I'm guessing it is, you're going to need a bit of help.' The Mercenary reasoned. It was sort of adorable... in a pathetic sort of way.

'You have one day.'

'What?' The Mercenary stopped struggling. Windera shuffled uncomfortably, sniffing her face to make sure she had not accidentally killed her.

'One day until that curse ends your pathetic little existence.' The Sorcerer sang, smiling.

'What curse?'

'The curse you caught sometime this morning. You really need to learn your spells. I can practically smell it on you.'

'Can't you break it?'

'No.'

'But-'

'No.' the Sorcerer snapped. 'It can only be broken by the one who set it - Jadella, or her servant, I'm guessing. You have until dawn.'

Somewhere between rage and panic, the Mercenary gasped 'Why didn't you mention this earlier?!'

'It wasn't my problem then.' The Sorcerer inspected her staff for a moment, running her fingers up and down the wood. Then she glanced back at the Mercenary, 'Now it is. You have approximately 22 hours until it takes effect. Which means you have 22 hours to tell me where Jadella is hiding.'

'If I tell you you'll just kill me.' The Sorcerer nodded – that sounded about right. The Mercenary, to her credit, kept trying. 'How about we work together. We find the cure, wake up Jadella and force her to save me. Then we fight it out, and whoever wins gets to keep her and her powers. Sound fair?'

'Not remotely. A fight between you and I? You don't stand a chance.' Grinning, the Sorcerer pictured the Mercenary skewered beneath her staff, Jadella's power flowing through her. This could work.

'Then what have you got to lose? I'm dead unless we wake her, and you can't find her without me.'

'True enough.'

'Then release me!' The Mercenary demanded, then continued a tad more calmly, 'I won't try anything.'

Nodding, the Sorcerer waved her hand again and Windera withdrew, lingering at a safe distance. The Mercenary stood, trying to regain what little dignity she had, 'So what do we need for this potion?'

'Oh a few simple things,' with a knowing wink, the Sorcerer turned away. She quickly located the scroll amid a pile of others. She stretched out the scroll in both hands and began to read aloud. 'Tongue of dragon, tear of Elf. Hound claws and sand from a... beach.'

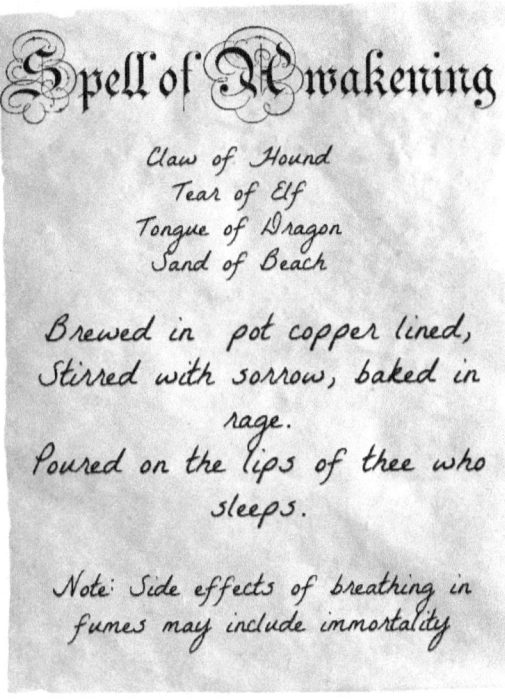

Spell of Awakening

Claw of Hound
Tear of Elf
Tongue of Dragon
Sand of Beach

Brewed in pot copper lined,
Stirred with sorrow, baked in rage.
Poured on the lips of thee who sleeps.

Note: Side effects of breathing in fumes may include immortality

The Mercenary was remarkably unimpressed, 'Sand from a beach?'

'Yes.'

'Seriously?'

'Shut up,' the Sorcerer snapped indignantly 'it's a potion, it's not all mystical hoo-doo.'

'If you say so.'

'I do.'

'Good.' The Mercenary sighed, 'Then are we going to get started? It's not like we have forever. We should split up, tell me where to get the ah... sand from a beach and Elf tear.'

'And dragon's tongue. I'm so not going to be the one getting that.' Mused the Sorcerer, 'Besides, the closest one I know of lives at the Whispering Shores; it's only three hours ride from the dwelling of the nearest Elf I know of. It makes sense for you to knock three off in one round trip.'

'So you get one ingredient and I get three. Remind me, how is this fair?' The Mercenary scowled, kicking the ground. A stone flew off into the bushes, and Windera scurried after it. The Mercenary raised an eyebrow.

'It's fair because if we succeed, you get to live.' The Sorcerer shrugged, 'Maybe.'

'Oh yay.'

'Smile Mercenary, you're about to meet one of the fairest creatures in all the worlds.'

'Whatever. Where is this Elf?'

The Sorcerer pointed to the North, 'Follow the path that way, you can't miss her.' Windera scurried out of the shadows, dropping the stone at the Mercenary's feet. 'Oh and take Windera, she'll keep an eye on you. Can't have you hatching any plans can we?'

Windera looked like she had just won a pot of gold; the Mercenary looked like she had just had one dropped on her head. Without a word, the two figures hurried away into the undergrowth in the direction the Sorcerer had pointed.

The Sorcerer spun on her heels. Hound claws would be no worries; she had a stash of them on her desk. Besides, she could use this time to prepare for the coming battle. The Mercenary with No Name would cause her no trouble – she could dispatch the fiend without breaking a sweat. Jadella, on the other hand, could be interesting.

Chapter 4

nessaria

Sun beams scorched the forest canopy; where they hit the leaves were alight with a golden glow. Corresponding patches of ground were almost blinding in contrast with the dark, morning air. The Elf rolled her shoulders. There! A rustle in the bushes. This was going to be fun. Really fun. Oh so so... yeah, you get the point.

With lightning speed, Nessaria raced forward onto a mound of dirt. She kneeling, she pulled an arrow from her quiver. She pulled back her bowstring. She blew hair out of her face. She took a breath... she shot.

The arrow whistled through the air, deadly as a viper... and sadly, even less straight. The arrow thudded uselessly into the leaf litter a good four metres from her target. With a huff, Nessaria stood and made her way towards it. She was meant to be an Elf. She was meant to be awesome. She was meant to be able to shoot a freaking bow and arrow.

Another rustle. Pulled from her thoughts, Nessaria shrunk into the foliage; her bow still in her hand, her arrows reachable in a second should she need them. She took a step forward. Beyond the tree-line, a woman was strolling along with a strange creature. A very strange creature, with fur and teeth and claws and... well, general weirdness. It was almost human-like, but smaller, with longer limbs and a face which resembled a dragon-hound hybrid. Yet it was wearing clothing - very strange. The woman was also a little odd; she had a brown stained cloak and... was that a sword? Nessaria lent closer, her face almost at the edge of the trees. Just a little closer... she was sure that was a-

She lost her balance and with the dignity of a drunken dragon, she tumbled forward. Smashing into the woman. The too-skinny creature looked over at the two figures in surprise, and began giggling manically – a strange noise to hear from such a wild creature.

Nessaria quickly jumped to her feet, 'Oh my bubbles I am so sorry! I didn't see you there. Here, come on get up.' She tried to offer the woman a hand, but it was swatted away, 'Are you alright?'

Glaring, the woman stood and placed a hand on what Nessaria was now certain was a sword, 'I'm fine. Who are you?'

Nessaria backed away, almost falling into the bushes again.

'I'm Nessaria, healer Elf of the Kelkarri forests. Though strictly speaking I'm still in training. But then again I don't actually have a conglomeration any more 'cause they all left but really that's not my fault. So I'm technically the ruler of my own non-'

'For the love of the Gods shut up!' The woman – who Nessaria now decided deserved the title of Mrs Grumps – interrupted and removed her hand from the hilt of her sword. Nessaria drew a silent breath, glancing over at the skinny monster. It had found her arrow and was happily chewing on it. 'I am here on behalf of the great Jadella of legend.' Mrs Grumps continued, regaining Nessaria's attention, 'She has fallen victim to a terrible poison-'

Nessaria gasped. 'Oh my that's terrible! What can I do to help? There has to be something. I once had an aunt that could-'

Again the woman interrupted 'I need to collect several ingredients to cure her, one of which you can provide me-'

'Sure! Sure anything! I have a tonne of healing stuff at my cabin; potions, elixirs, herbs, potatoes... not that you would really need potatoes, that would be silly. Although my great grand-'

'I need a tear! That's all!' Mrs Grumps snapped, waving her hands irritably at Nessaria as though resisting the urge to simultaneously slap and strangle her.

Nessaria tilted her head to the side, trying not to take offence. This was odd, even by her standards. 'A tear? Are you sure? That's rather weird. And odd. Although... hang on, do you mean one of my tears?'

'What else would I mean?'

'Well-'

'Nevermind.' The woman turned away, watching as

her demonic companion began burying Nessaria's arrow. 'Just one Elven tear is all I need. Are you willing to oblige?'

Nessaria tried to keep the suspicion out of her voice, 'Sure sure, of course!' With a grin she began poking herself around the eyes, 'Hmmm, I know there's one here somewhere... You know, my mother had this technique where she-'

'I don't care. I need a tear, not a story.' Without breaking eye contact, the woman grasped the hilt of her sword. 'Now are you going to give it to me or do you want a hand?'

Nessaria giggled nervously, 'That won't be necessary. Torture takes way too long and we elves can be very stubborn. I had an uncle that survived over three years in the prison of the Sphinx Ego, nasty stuff that. Tell you what, I'll come with you on your journey and then, when you have all the ingredients I'll be so happy that I'll cry!'

The skinny monster looked up at her, tilting her head curiously as if to say "what the heck is wrong with this maniac?"

'No way. I'm not taking you with me.' Mrs Grumps seemed to cringe at the thought. 'I have only a few hours to get the ingredients I need - you'll just slow me down.'

'But I'm not sad now!' Nessaria pressed, 'I can't shed tears when I'm not sad.'

The woman shook her head slowly, appearing as though she was attempting to resist the urge to murder Nessaria in some bloody, violent manner. 'Look, I have had a very long, very irritating day. I don't have time of this.'

'Exactly! Take me with you! I haven't had an adventure in sooo long. Please? Pleeaassee? Pleeeaaasssee?'Nessaria whined, eyes bulging.

'I'm really starting to see why your family left you.' Commented Mrs Grumps dryly.

Crossing her arms, Nessaria huffed, 'Well aren't you a mean little bee.' Then once more she was grinning, 'So where to now? Huh huh? Oh I know! Drake Lake! Or... The Belthvonian Doorway. Yeah that's meant to have-'

'The beach. We're going to the beach. Do you have horses?'

Grinning, Nessaria replied, 'I have a unicorn.'

Apparently Mrs Grumps was also Mrs Sceptic, 'I'll take that as a no then.' She sighed, then pats Nessaria on the back and pushed her forward along the path. 'Come on, it's a long walk, but if we're lucky we'll find some horses to steal on our way.'

Nessaria glanced at the woman, trying to hide her concern. She had helped Jadella in the past; she and her maid were good friends. It seemed odd that they would recruit someone so violent to help them, no matter how bad things were. No, something was definitely wrong here.

Feeling a new surge of Elfish-bravery swell inside of her, she allowed herself to be led along the winding path. The skinny creature scurried just behind them, sniffing at the various trees and flowers they passed.

Chapter 5

dragon's tongue

They walked for hours. It was hot, and dull, and the Mercenary with No Name was ready to kill something. More than ready, she was eager to. She could not wait to feel her blade sink into the Sorcerer's gut, hear the flesh tear and watch the blood ooze. It would be sublime.

But first, she needed to collect the last of the ingredients. This meant having to put up with Nessaria's endless flurry of stories – most of which she could not even follow. If only she had the time to torture the tears out of her. But the stupid Elf was right; there was no way she could do it in the limited time she had.

'Hang on, you still haven't told me your name.' Nessaria said suddenly, 'I forgot to ask, how very rude of me. What's your name? Do you have a name? Oh don't be silly Nessaria everyone has a name. So what is it? Huh?'

Remaining stubbornly silent, the Mercenary kicked a rock on the heavily-treed path. She watched as it slowly tumbled along the rocks and fallen branches before disappearing down the steep slope of the forest. Windera followed it over.

'Oh come on, you can tell me!' Nessaria continued at her usual pace, 'Please? Come on. Name! Name! Name! Name!'

she began chanting, leaning close to the Mercenary. Too close.

Without thinking, the Mercenary swung a punch at the Elf. Nessaria yelped and ducked. The power behind the Mercenary's punch – with the aid of an inconveniently placed branch – pulled her forwards. Usually she was an excellent warrior, but exhaustion and irritation got the better of her and she landed flat on her face. Nessaria was squished beneath her. To add insult to injury, Windera chose that exact moment to come barreling back out of the forest. She joined the pile with a satisfied grunt.

'Get off!' The Mercenary growled, kicking her away. She rolled off and squatted, grinning manically. The Mercenary groaned. Nessaria was sprawled across the path; her head flopped to the side next to a large rock. Her eyes were closed.

'Great.' Clenching her fists, the Mercenary stood and glanced around. 'Look what you did,' the Mercenary scolded, pointing from Windera to Nessaria. Windera scratched behind her ear, picked something from the matted fur and shoved it in her mouth. 'And now I'm talking to a... whatever the hell you are.' Windera snorted, giving no indication she understood. Every part of the Mercenary being wanted to stab the Elf and the ghoul, and leave them in the dirt for the griffins to feast on. But they were needed.

The Elf was only unconscious for a short while, just long enough for the Mercenary to build a basic sled to drag her along on. She would not have bothered, only it was quicker for her to tug a sled than drag an unconscious body with long limbs that caught on every branch and rock they could find (speaking from experience, of course). But just as she was about to load the idiot onto the sled, the idiot woke up and began chattering about how pretty the trees were. Typical.

Several hours later they had almost reached the supposed location of the dragon. Nessaria said she had heard of the creature from some villagers, so knew where it was. More or less. The Elf threw a stick for Windera as they strolled along the sand; the Mercenary had long since given up telling them to hurry. Windera was almost comical in the way she smashed head-first into the waves after the stick, but the Mercenary did not laugh. Nessaria did. It was extremely annoying.

Finally they reached the Whispering Shores, located just before the mouth of the Ki'larian river. Twisting trees curled upwards from the ground, their roots thrust deep into the water like straws. The roaring wind was the only sound (besides Nessaria) in the apparently desolate landscape.

'Are we there yet?' whined Nessaria, dragging her exhausted feet to a rest beside the Mercenary. Shooting Nessaria a glare, the Mercenary scanned the horizon. Windera bounded ahead of them and disappeared into the trees.

'According to the Sorcerer the dragon's lair is somewhere in this vicinity. We should fan out. You go down along the beach and I'll go forest-side.' she said, pointing towards the water, then the forest. 'Here, take this and fill it with sand.' She continued, handing Nessaria an empty vial, 'No water, just sand. We need it for the potion.'

Nessaria nodded, grinning, 'Sure thing boss! I'm very good at gathering ingredients. I used to-'

The Mercenary held up a hand. Nessaria stopped talking. 'We are near the home of a very dangerous creature,' she patronised, 'You need to shut up, or it will rip your throat out. And that would be quite inconvenient, as we still need one of your tears.' Nessaria opened her mouth to reply, but the Mercenary silenced her again. 'Now, I'm betting that the dragon will be higher up on the rocks, but I can't know for sure. If you see it, you come and get me. Do not try and start a conversation, understand?'

Mercenary watched Nessaria skip away towards the water. The second the Elf was out of view, the infamous warrior slumped against the closest tree. 'Why couldn't this blasted potion call for the tongue of an Elf and tear of a dragon?' she moaned, 'At least then I wouldn't have to listen to that insufferable chatterbox.'

What was meant to be a quick snag, bag and cut out tongue operation proved to be far harder than expected; they could not even get past the first step. They had failed to 'acquire' horses on their journey, which had prolonged their trip to the beach by several hours. Now, even with the three of them, it took several hours to thoroughly search the beach, and by then the second sun was brushing the mountain tops. Still there was no sign of the beast.

Exasperated beyond belief, the Mercenary stormed over to Windera, who was digging in a pile of rocks. She pulled the creature roughly up by the arm and fixed it with a glare.

'Windera,' she said tensely, 'The dragon is not here. Is there any way we can contact the Sorcerer and get a more precise location?'

Windera tilted her head to the side, poking out her tongue to lick the fur around her chin. Her eyes were still focused on the pile of stones. The Mercenary shook her, barely resisting the urge to fling the skinny monster across the beach. Windera's attention finally fell upon her, and the creature let out an odd squealing noise. Then, with lightning speed, she tore free of the Mercenary's grasp and bolted into the bushes.

The Mercenary stomped the ground, flinging her arms into the air, 'Oh very helpful!' she called after the creature, 'what a waste of air.' She turned away. The land around them was quite spectacular; sparkling water lapped at the sunbaked shore, golden sand embraced the sea, puffy clouds bobbed around the baby blue sky. It was sickening. Where was the blood, the energy, the adventure? Where were the dragons? One could barely stay awake in such a serene place.

As if on cue, a strangled squawk shredded the peace. Windera came bounding out of the forest, a large greenish bird in hand. She skidded to a stop at the Mercenary's feet, holding the creature up to her. It looked terrified.

'What the hell is this?' the Mercenary exclaimed.

Windera shook the bird.

'Huh?'

Windera shook it again.

'Not helpful.' The Mercenary snatched the bird, holding it around the back to prevent it from flapping. Windera grabbed at the bird's feet.

'What are you doing with a Forest Flier?' Nessaria popped up suddenly from behind a tree, 'I didn't know they lived here. Those things are rare. Really rare. Really really...'

'What does it do?' interrupted the Mercenary, handing her the struggling creature.

Nessaria hugged it, 'They're used to send messages. How do you not know that?' The bird seemed to calm, as though appreciative of her comfort and understanding.

'Well then,' said the Mercenary, patting Windera on the back, 'That is exactly what we need to do. I want to contact a Sorcerer friend of mine who might have some idea of the dragon's location. Can you do this for me?'

Nessaria nodded enthusiastically. She placed the bird on the ground and plucked a feather from its tail; she then proceeded to grab a dead leaf from the ground, and a flat rock. With a flourish, she began scratching runes into the leaf with the feather. The rock provided a flat backing while she worked. It took only a few minutes, but felt like hours to the Mercenary.

Finally she stood, piercing the leaf with the feather. The bird looked up at her curiously. Nessaria smiled softly, leaning down to return the feather – leaf still attached – to the bird's tail. It seemed to grow back into the green plumage and the bird stood erect. Then suddenly it was off, bounding away into the forest.

The Mercenary stared at Nessaria. The Elf grinned, 'There you go.'

'So it's going to the Sorcerer?'

'Yes.'

'But how does it know where to go?'

Nessaria frowned, 'It's psychic stupid.'

'So there was a bird reading my mind?' The Mercenary growled, but she was too tired to question further. 'When will it return?'

'Soon. Well, pretty soon. Probably. Depends how fast it is, and how fast your Sorcerer is at responding. We should get back to searching.' Nessaria skipped back down to the sand, leaving Windera and the Mercenary alone on the rocks.

'Well done.' Nodding awkwardly to Windera, the Mercenary continued back to the other end of river mouth. Time to campus the area… again.

After another hour, the Mercenary was definitely ready to light the whole beach on fire and smoke the dragon out of wherever it was hiding. Hell, she was ready to blow the place up! What sort of dragon could stay hidden on a tiny little beach without being found – it was not like there were any spooky caves for it to conceal itself in.

Rubbing her forehead in exhaustion, the Mercenary allowed herself to sit for a moment on a relatively shaded spot. Nessaria, much to her dismay, plonked beside her. 'Argh, this is taking way too long.' The Mercenary groaned.

Nessaria glanced at the sky, 'It's not that late.' She commented, somehow retaining her cheery tone despite all that had happened, 'We have a little while until dark-time. How about we call it quits and make camp. I have this wonderful idea for a meal involving-'

'We don't have time.' Replied the Mercenary, 'We have to find this freaking dragon and get back to Jadella tonight.'

'But why? What's wrong with her exactly? Is it some sort of timer thing? Where she dies after three days or something? But then you wouldn't want to be back by tonight...' she held up a finger triumphantly as though a genius idea had occurred to her. She quickly reached into her pocket and pulled out a small glass vial, 'Oh by the way here's your sand.'

The Mercenary's heart sunk; for a second she had dared to hope the useless Elf had some way of getting them out of this predicament. She took the vial and continued staring at the waves. 'We have one day,' she explained, 'I- she dies when the third sun rises tomorrow. We need to get back well before then. Which means-'

Suddenly Windera came scurrying over the rocks towards them. Her face was masked in terror; strange squealing noises emanated from her mouth. As she reached them, the Mercenary caught her around the shoulders, stopping her in her tracks.

'Whoa there, stop. Stop,' the Mercenary commanded, 'You're going to give away our position.' The Mercenary frowned, staring at the Sorcerer's minion suspiciously. Then her face was replaced by the back of Nessaria's head as she leant between them.

'It's trying to say something.' The Elf commented, peering at the creature. 'Hello? What are you saying?' she said to Windera, before looking back at the Mercenary, 'She looks scared, what do you think it saw? 'Again she turned to the creature, 'What did you see? Was it a unicorn? Are you alright? Did you hurt yourself? Are you okay?'

Pushing her head away, the Mercenary snapped, 'Not

helping.' She took a deep breath, 'Okay Windera, calm down. What did you see? Was it another bunny?'

'Um...'Nessaria interrupted.

'Not now.'

'Ah no yeah, this is sort of important.' Nessaria's voice was quaking a little, 'I know what she saw.'

Frowning, the Mercenary turned to her. Nessaria was pointing at the ground before her. The Mercenary followed her gaze to see a miniature dragon, about the size of a melon, staring up at them. It was adorable, with big eyes and tiny horns; if not for the burning desire to save her own skin, the Mercenary may have thought twice about killing it.

'Oh.' The Mercenary remarked, 'Well, looks like we've found our dragon.' Releasing Windera, she drew her sword. With a flourish, she aimed the tip at the dragon and smiled.

The dragon took a frightened step back, but its back was pressed against a wall of tangled roots and branches.

'What are you doing?' exclaimed Nessaria, stepping between them, 'Don't do that! Leave it alone.'

'Step aside Elf. Let me do what we came here for.' growled the Mercenary, still aiming the blade at the small creature. Windera cowered pathetically behind her.

'You came here to kill it!? What? But- But it's just a baby!'

'Yeah, I'm going to kill it. Welcome to the human race, we kill things.'

The Elf's horror changed to determination, 'I can't let you do this.' She looked around for a moment, then snatched up a stick from a tree. Swallowing hard, she aimed it at the Mercenary. She was quivering like a leaf; what a joke. Nessaria slapped the Mercenary's sword with the stick, shuffling further between her and the dragon.

The Mercenary was torn. If she killed the Elf, she would not get her tear. If she let the Elf live, she may not get the dragon. She took a step back, allowing the Elf to scoop up the dragon. It trembled in her arms. So much for the fearsome dragon of the Whispering Shores.

Nessaria swung her stick again, 'I won't let you harm it! Stay back!'

The Mercenary reached forward casually and snatched the stick from her. Nessaria quickly grabbed another, shorter one. The Mercenary took this also, and threw it into the ocean. Windera ran after it. Nessaria backed away, climbing higher on the rocks with the dragon.

'Give it to me!' commanded the Mercenary.

Nessaria shook her head, 'What do you want it for anyway? It's just a baby! You can't harm an itty little baby can you?'

Resisting the urge to point out that yes, in fact, she would gladly gut the creature, the Mercenary replied, 'The potion calls for hound claws, beach sand, Elf's tear and dragon's tongue. I have everything else I need. Just give me the dragon. Jadella's life depends on it.'

Nessaria almost dropped the dragon. 'Dragon's tongue?' she exclaimed, 'But I have one of those! Back at my cabin, with all my other ingredients.'

Now the Mercenary really felt like killing her, 'Why didn't you mention this earlier? Why does no one mention these things earlier?' she kicked the sand, spraying Nessaria with grit.

'I did!'

'No you didn't.'

'Did too. I said I had lots of helpful stuff!' the Elf sounded hurt.

'But you didn't say you had a dragons tongue!'

'You didn't ask!'

The Mercenary looked away, clenching her jaw in frustration. This was without doubt the worst, most ridiculous and mind-numbingly frustrating day she had ever endured. Why had she not simply intercepted Jadella on the road, before she got past her magical barrier? True, she probably would have died in the fight against such a powerful Sorcerer, but at this stage that seemed a far better alternative.

'Fine. Whatever.' With a sigh, the Mercenary sheathed her sword. She nodded up at Nessaria. Windera had returned with the stick and was sitting on the rocks beside them chewing it. 'Let's head back to your cabin then, it's on our way anyway. But bring that thing with you.' She pointed to the dragon, 'If you're lying, I'm going to want a backup. Okay?'

Nessaria grinned, 'It's a deal!' She jumped to her feet and strode back the way they had come. The Mercenary turned to follow but the Elf suddenly spun on her heals. She stuck out her bottom lip and bulged her eyes. It took a second for the Mercenary to realise she was begging for something.

'What now?'

'Can we maybe just... you know, sleep a little first? It's been a really long day and I'm so tired!'

'Did you not hear me earlier? Jadella dies at the dawn of the third sun!' Maybe it would be simpler if the Mercenary just killed herself now.

'I know, but I can't continue like this. Just a few hours. Besides, if you want a tear from me you need me to be happy... wait no, that doesn't make sense. You need me to be sad, and I will be sad if we sleep so you should let us. Come on, please?'

The Mercenary could barely believe her ears, 'Are you trying to extort me?'

'No... well a little. You need me, and I need sleep. So yeah I guess I am.' She said defiantly.

'Fine.' replied the Mercenary after several seconds of glaring, 'When it gets dark, you can have a few hours. Until then let's keep moving. Bring the dragon.'

Chapter 6

wings of windera

Darkness was lovely. It was black and sweet and calm and quiet and oh so beautiful. It was the time she felt most at home. It was the time she thrived and hunted and ran and killed. It was her very essence spilling into the world.

Or at least, it might have been. But Windera never thought like that. She did not think much of anything really. Darkness was the same as lightness, only it was harder to see. Sweet was a taste, not a feeling. Calm was boring. Quiet was lack of noise. Night was just dark.

Not tonight though, tonight they had a fire. It was warm. Her mistress's enemy was sitting on a log, cleaning something sharp. Something she wanted. The other one - the one that talked - was sleeping with the small monster they had caught at the sandy place. She was hugging it. She was still talking, but Windera could not understand the words.

The enemy was tired. Her strokes were slowing, her eyes were drooping. Windera watched her. Windera smiled. Night was for sleeping, and that is what they were doing. This was her chance. The enemy yawned, placing her sharp thing in its holder on the log beside her. She slowly closed her eyes...

Windera wasted no time. Silently, she scurried onto the log next to the enemy. Her fingers darted forward, snatching at the end of the sharp thing. She slid it silently from its holder, and disappeared into the darkness.

Windera ran. Far and fast; she had to get away. She had to return to her mistress. In one hand she grasped the enemy's weapon. The other she used, with the aid of her legs, to race along the forest floor. Her mistress had commanded her. She was to bring her the enemy's sharp thing. The enemy could not know.

When she was far enough away and her legs began to tire, she climbed high into the branches of a tall tree. The sharp thing nearly cut her many times. At the top, she took a moment to breathe. The Senthai moons had travelled high into the night sky. It had been a while since she had left, and the enemy would now have woken. She had to hurry.

Windera used the sharp thing to slice the back of her clothes; two long slits from the collar to about two thirds down her back. She lifted her head to the sky and breathed in the night air. Then, sharp thing in hand, she threw herself from the branches of the tree. She had almost hit the ground when her wings unfurled. Thin and leathery, they carried her high into the sky. The sword weighed her down a little, but not enough to slow her advance.

Chapter 7

midnight melody

'This is not a shortcut!' Mrs Grumps groaned, punching a poor, innocent shrub on her way past.

Nessaria rolled her eyes, unseen by Mrs Grumps in the pitch blackness, 'Yes it is! I told you, you can get to my cabin much faster by travelling through the Kelkarri forests, rather than around them. Honestly, what's the worst that can happen?'

'Oh you did not just say that.'

Nessaria paused, looking again at the sky. She had intended to use the moons as a guide on their journey home, just as she had often done on her late-night expeditions. Unfortunately, she had forgotten to take into account the thick canopy of the forest in this part. The moons were almost entirely out of sight. 'We'll be fine.' She assured her companion, 'As long as we stay out of Midnight Melody territory, nothing can go wrong.'

Mrs Grumps sounded like she would choke, 'Midnight Melodies? I thought they were Belthvon's problem! Since when do they live here?' The dragon, curled in Nessaria's arms like a child, stirred slightly in its sleep. Mrs Grumps had insisted it was muzzled and tied with griffin feather ropes – an unbreakable bond – and tethered to

Nessaria's wrist.

'Something to do with the war.' Nessaria replied, 'I think they came here after Belthvon fell into anarchy. You know, they say the war will likely come here next, but the Reather Egos are still trying to contain it.'

Nessaria knew little of the goings on of the other worlds. The doorways that joined the land had been open for many years, but few travelled through. Legend had it there were powerful forces at work over there, gods and Egos fighting against one another to seize control of the four planets. Jadella was probably the only one that could stop it - if she used her powers. Nessaria doubted her friend ever would.

Suddenly the Elf realised that her companion had not responded. Mrs Grumps was not the most talkative person, but they had been mid-conversation. She should have replied. Then Nessaria realised. She had stopped talking too. She had stopped moving. She was lying on the ground, half buried in the carpet of leaves. The Dragon was tugging gently against its tether. A beautiful melody was floating around the forest, teasing Nessaria's mind back towards the darkness. It was so calming, so tempting...

But Nessaria knew better.

'Wake up!' she spluttered, choking on leaves. She kicked out wildly, hitting something hard. The hard thing groaned and muttered something about stabbing her eyes out. 'Move!' Nessaria shouted again. Her arms were numb, but she managed to use them to rise a little. She flopped onto her side, gasping from the effort. The dragon, somehow immune to the song, nuzzled her shoulder as though urging her to continue. Midnight Melodies were all around them; their golden-tipped feathers seemed to glow like starlight. They had come out of nowhere. They were so beautiful, like tiny black and gold phoenixes. Their voices were soft, oozing through the air like honey - coating them, ensnaring them.

'We have to move.' The words were bitter in Nessaria's mouth. She hated to break the spell, but she knew they had to move. Jadella's life depended on it.

She forced herself to her feet, dragon in arms, and leant heavily against a tree. The Midnight Melodies glared down at her. Their eyes were like tiny fires burning into her. No longer did their song seem gentle and caring – now it was like children screaming, hell hounds snarling and thunder crashing all at once. Nessaria covered her ears, sinking back to the ground. They were preparing to feast. Nessaria had to do something – she did not want to be dinner!

Taking a deep breath, Nessaria pulled her bow and an arrow from her tangled hair. She aimed it at the nearest bird. Her arms shook; her mind fought to stay focused. She had to do this. A surge of bravery overtook her, as though a switch had been flicked. She was an Elf. She was healer and a warrior. She was freaking awesome. Nessaria armed the bow, pulled back the string, and shot…

And missed.

She tried again and missed. By the third attempt any sense of nobility and power had drained from her. She was useless. She could not win against these creatures.

'You know, I don't even know why I bother.' Nessaria snapped, flinging her bow to the ground. 'I am the most pathetic, stupid, underachieving Elf this side of Arbennig. I've never healed a wound, never hit a target, never saved the day! Even my family left me, driven away by my utter failure at life no doubt!' She slouched against the tree, crossing her arms over her chest. One of the Midnight Melodies fluttered down to her; it perched on her arm like a parrot. The dragon snarled at it, but did not attack.

'What's wrong with me?' she asked it. The bird whistled gently in response, trying to put her back under the spell. Midnight Melodies fed off flesh, but legend had it the purpose of their songs was to overwhelm their victims with feelings of hopelessness, sadness, regret - all sorts of yucky emotions Nessaria wanted nothing to do with. Maybe bad feelings make brains taste better. Right now she was a buffet just waiting to be savoured. Or maybe they were like sirens, only a lot less scaly. Either way they needed Nessaria to be subdued; active meals were more likely to run away than semi-conscious ones.

'Seriously, what on Senthai did I do to deserve this? I didn't hurt anyone... well, except for my brother. Funny story that...' the bird looked confused – this was not meant to happen. Meals were not meant to talk back. Yet on she went, explaining how she had accidently set a series off cabin defense mechanisms around her childhood home and caught her brother in one of them.

Another Midnight Melody joined the first, singing with all its might. 'You know, I had an aunt that could sing like that.' replied Nessaria. The bird did not protest her story, so she continued. She explained about her aunt's brief but spectacular singing career during which time she sung in villages all across the land. Until she was almost beheaded, that is.

By the time she had finished another eight had joined her on the ground. Like the first, they tried to subdue her with their sweet little songs – but Nessaria was on a roll. She told them of the exploits of various friends, family members and complete strangers. She absolutely loved telling stories, and for once she had an audience that did not protest. Well, not comprehensibly anyway. The dragon had covered its little ears with its wings and was growling softly at the new arrivals.

Nessaria was about to launch into the tale of the time her grandfather hunted a drake across the Arbennigian Glass Dessert when, in a flurry of talons and feathers, the birds dissipated. In seconds the air was clear of birdsong - apparently Nessaria was a little too much of a bother, especially when there was easier prey about. The only sign they had been there was a single gold tipped feather that slowly floated to the rainforest floor. As soon as it was in reach, the dragon jumped on it.

'Wha- what happened?' murmured a voice from within the shadows. Nessaria stood, gathering the dragon into her arms and returning her weapons to their quiver.

'Midnight Melodies,' Nessaria quickly explained what had happened, gently guiding Mrs Grumps to her feet. For once she did not protest.

'Then how are we alive?'

'They didn't like my stories.'

A horrid sound broke out from amid the foliage; it took

Nessaria a moment to realise it was the woman laughing. Several excruciating seconds later it ended as abruptly as it had begun, 'How long was I out?' Mrs Grumps demanded.

'I don't know. Not too long I think.' Nessaria tried once more to find the position of the moons.

'We need to get moving.' Mrs Grumps snapped, continuing forward.

Chapter 8

sorcerer's secrets

The Sorcerer gently caressed the cockatrice's feathery head, sliding her fingers between its horns. It nudged her hand, adjusting her position to suit its preferred patting spot. It was so small, so cute. Slowly, the Sorcerer slid a knife from its sheath and positioned it against the cockatrice's scaly throat.

'This won't hurt a bit,' she whispered, gently sliding it beneath the scales. The cockatrice remained calm, entranced by her touch, as the knife sunk deeper and deeper. Carefully the Sorcerer twisted the blade, chipping away at the dirt beneath the scales until there was none left.

'See, that wasn't so hard, was it?' Sheathing the knife, she moved her fingers around the scratch its chin. The cockatrice snorted, shuffling out of her reach. Sitting back against a tree, the Sorcerer watched it swoop over the trees and out of sight.

Most cockatrice were fussy when it came to personal grooming, this little one was the exception. He was constantly getting dirt and gosh knows what else under his scales and in his feathers. At least this time it was not something caught in his beak; the Sorcerer almost lost a finger the last time.

In her mind, the Sorcerer could feel Windera's thoughts racing about. She had met a new friend – probably an Elf based on her description – and was on her way home. The Sorcerer had little patience for elves, or any humanoid for that matter. She would much rather spend time with the beasts of Senthai and beyond. But of course, this was rather hard to achieve when they were being hunted like monsters. If humanity kept spreading at its current rate, the worlds would be overcome. No creature would be left unscathed. No creatures would be left at all.

The only person that could stop the bloodshed was Jadella. Yet being human herself, she stubbornly refused. If only the Sorcerer could gain her powers. She would end the slaughter of her friends once and for all. The humans would pay for what they had done to this beautiful land. She would destroy them all.

Windera landed in an explosion of leaves on the forest floor. The Sorcerer looked up, smiling as her minion scurried quickly to her mistress's side. With a little bow, Windera handed her the Mercenary's weapon.

The Sorcerer smiled, patting her gingerly on the head, 'Well done Windera. You have done very well.' She rubbed her hands on her shawl to remove the oily grime from her fingertips. Windera should probably have spent a little longer in the water when she had the chance – she was even dirtier than the Forest Flier that had come squawking to the Sorcerer earlier. The Sorcerer had ignored the bird's message of course; it would not pay to expedite her rival's journey. She needed the Mercenary at her very weakest if her plan was to work.

'Oh dear, what have you done to your dress?' The Sorcerer exclaimed, flicking the wings protruding from the two tears in Windera's garment, 'You've ruined it!' Windera looked up guiltily, folding her wings back inside the tattered fabric. With a flick of the Sorcerer's hands, the threads re-joined.

'Now,' the Sorcerer continued, 'we have work to do. Did they collect the other ingredients?' Windera shook her head. The Sorcerer frowned. Windera explained the situation in a series of grunts and squeals, tearing at the air with her talons.

'So they are going back to the Elf's cabin to get the tongue. Good, then they will not have to kill a dragon.'

Windera squeaked, expressing her concerns – what if she had taken too long, what if the Mercenary had realised the sword was gone or killed the dragon anyway.

With a sigh, she gathered her belongings, 'I sent some birds to watch them in your place, and if need be, slow them while you came to me.'

Windera still looked worried. She wanted more than anything to please her mistress. Her mistress was kind to her; everyone else – except that strange Elf – treated her like a beast. The Sorcerer knelt beside her, stroking the side of her head, 'You did well, Windera. Do not worry. We will make the potion and save Jadella; then you and all your kind will finally be free.'

Windera snorted satisfactorily and began licking the grime between her toes. Smiling, the Sorcerer stood. 'They should be at the cabin by now. We shall meet them there and teleport the rest of the way. If this is to work, timing is paramount.' She took one last look at her home. The skulls of creatures past, the spell books and potions; this was her own little sanctuary for all the creatures under her protection. The fate of everything that the Sorcerer had worked so hard to build was reliant on her achieving her goal. She hoped she would see them again.

Chapter 9

cabin in the woods

Crash! Another jar smashed to the floor, soaking the Mercenary's boots with an unidentified liquid. Something squirmed from within the shards, slowly making its way over her ankle. The Mercenary cringed, kicking whatever it was away; she really did not want to know what lay in the depths of this Elf's cabin.

'I know it's here somewhere!' Nessaria called for the umpteenth time, 'I had it out just the other day. Oh come on, here tonguey tonguey tonguey.' Something else fell to the ground with a dry thud.

Squinting, the Mercenary backed against a wall. 'Can't we get some light?'

'But I thought we were in a hurry! If I stop to find the candles, then light them so I can find the dragon's tongue, then it'll take even longer! Unless of course...'

'Nevermind.' The Mercenary snapped. The dragon was in her arms now, allowing the Nessaria the freedom to search for the final ingredient. It was a cute little fella, but the Mercenary wanted nothing more than to slit its throat. Instead she satisfied herself with saying, 'Just hurry okay.'

They had finally made their way back to Nessaria's cabin. Thankfully they had encountered no more Midnight Melodies on their trip. She thought it odd the hellish birds had appeared just as they had been discussing them, and even stranger that they had been so easily dispatched. The Mercenary tried not put too much thought into it - she was far too tired to care.

A sudden flash dissipated her thoughts. Blinded, the Mercenary lurched forward, tipping over a bench. Cups and saucers filled with all manner of junk clattered across the floor. The Mercenary struggled to keep the startled dragon in her arms as it flapped and lashed out. Somewhere in the room, Nessaria yelped.

After a few seconds the light faded and they were plunged into darkness. 'What was that?' The Mercenary blinked, trying to regain her bearings.

'I don't know.' Nessaria's face appeared beside her own, lit by a flickering candle.

The Mercenary raised an eyebrow, 'What are you doing?'

'I found a candle.'

'I can see that.' Slinging the dragon further up on her shoulder, the Mercenary shuffled away from the tiny light.

'It was in a box, with the tongue.' Nessaria explained. She held up a large jar, its contents silhouetted against the light of the candle.

For the first time all day, the Mercenary's heart soared. She practically threw the dragon back to Nessaria, snatching the jar from her hand. This was it. She had it. Only one ingredient left… 'Well done.' She smiled cruelly, gesturing towards the door, 'Now shall we?'

As if on cue, there was a knocking at the door. The Mercenary looked to Nessaria; the Elf just shrugged. Turning back to the door, the Mercenary frowned. The knocking continued. Cautiously, she walked towards the sound, her hand resting just above her scabbard. She opened the door and stepped outside.

Light flooded the forest, emanating from the Sorcerer's upturned palms; Windera was at her feet picking at the leaf-covered ground. Slowly the Sorcerer turned to face them, eyes still glowing. It was as though morning had already arrived. Swallowing a growing sense of dread, the Mercenary stepped aside, allowing Nessaria to squeeze past with the dragon. The Elf hurriedly placed the small creature on the ground and nudged it towards the bushes, 'Farewell little one, good luck!' Shooting a nervous glance towards the Sorcerer, the dragon scuttled away.

Nessaria stood, frowning at the Sorcerer. She seemed unsure whether to run or kneel. One day the Mercenary would have that sort of respect. 'Cool trick. How are you generating it?' The infamous warrior called, breaking the silence.

With a sly smile, the Sorcerer mused, 'The light? It's magic, Mercenary. That's what I'm here for.' her smile disappeared, 'You, on the other hand, are little more than a nuisance. What took you so long anyway? Windera came running back to me hours ago saying you ditched her.' She gestured to the pouting creature at her feet.

'We took a short cut.' snapped the Mercenary, glaring at Nessaria.

The Elf looked indignant, 'Well it's not my fault! How was I to know the Midnight Melodies hunt at night? Really, it's not like I could have helped it. Wait...' she faltered. Finally reality had penetrated her thick skull, 'you're a Mercenary?'

Raising a hand to silence her, the Mercenary groaned to the Sorcerer, 'See what I have had to put up with. She wouldn't give me the tear until we found the other ingredients. Figured I didn't have enough time torture it out of her. But for you it shouldn't be too hard.' The Sorcerer nodded, 'Now shall we get to Jadella? I don't have much time.'

'What? What do you mean? Who are you?' Nessaria had gone snow white. She began to edge away, but was just a little too slow.

With a grunt, the Mercenary punched her in the face, 'Shut up!' Nessaria fell dazed to the ground.

The Sorcerer walked up to them calmly, peering down at Nessaria. Her eyes narrowed for a second and then looked back at her ally. 'Calm down, we have a job to do.' She grabbed the Elf's wrist gently and placed a hand on the Mercenary's forehead. Windera scurried up to them, grabbing the Sorcerer around the ankles. 'Now think of where Jadella lies.' The Sorcerer whispered, 'Take us to her.' In a whirl of sparks, the world shattered; for several seconds, the only light emanated from the eyes of the Sorcerer. Then only darkness remained.

Chapter 10

final battle

When the light returned they were somewhere else. A long grey sand bank, sprinkled with rotten wood and various grasses that jutted from the dunes. Rainforest provided a little shade on one side of the bank; the other side consisted of a steep drop into a murky creek. It took a moment for the Mercenary to realise that they were on the other side of Jadella's hovel. The first sun was poking its ugly head over the tree tops; the others would not be far behind. She glared at the Sorcerer suspiciously, but instead of making a move to attack, the witch just smiled.

'Remember our deal. Make the cure, then we fight. I think we have about ten minutes till the third sun rises.'

The Sorcerer nodded, 'Have a little faith.' She leant down to Nessaria, who was pinned down by Windera with her mouth covered by two grimy hands, 'Now come on dear, just one little tear.' Eyes glowing, the Sorcerer summoned a tear to bubble up from the Elf's eye – she caught it easily in a vial and withdrew.

She then pulled out a golden pot and tipped the tear in, followed by a large curved claw that clinked as it hit the bottom. 'And the other ingredients?' The Sorcerer turned to look at the Mercenary, 'I trust you were able to acquire them.'

Still maintaining her stoic glare, the Mercenary handed

her the sand and tongue. The Sorcerer took a moment to relish in the gore of the bloody pink tongue before letting it splosh into the now fizzing brew. Where the liquid content had come from, the Mercenary would never know. Finally the Sorcerer snatched one of the arrows from Nessaria's tangled hair and stirred the potion.

'So,' she said after a moment, 'tell me Mercenary, while we wait for this to brew, why is it you chose to hunt our dear friend Jadella?'

Taken aback, the Mercenary snorted, 'Why do you care?'

'I'm just curious as to why a lowly Mercenary would suddenly decide to take fate into their own hands. Ruling the world is quite a task you know.' The Sorcerer replied, slowly standing.

'Who says I want to rule it? I just wanted to take it. Pay back some old debts, that sort of thing.' She took a deep breath, somehow overcome with the urge to spill her guts to the woman. In hindsight, it was probably some sort of spell. 'My parents-'

'Mummy and daddy issues? Seriously?' The Sorcerer chuckled, 'Well isn't that the old cliché. I suppose Jadella's power was meant to make them treat you better?' She stepped closer to the Mercenary, her nose only inches away, 'She can't change the past you know.' The Mercenary really, really wanted to stab her in the face. But who knew how complicated the rest of the curing process was going to be; the potion may only be half finished and the Sorcerer was the only one who could make it.

Instead she resigned herself to saying, 'It's more complicated than that.'

'Isn't it always?'

'And you? What are your motives?'

'I'm just doing this for fun.' She peered at the pot sideways and smiled. Leaning down, she continued, 'And we're done.'

All at once, Nessaria shoved Windera and launched to her feet; the creature fell squealing onto the sand for a moment before giving chase. The Mercenary saw her chance; the Sorcerer was distracted. She lunged.

'Goodbye Sorcerer!' The Sorcerer fell backwards under the Mercenary's weight, barely missing a tangled scrawl of branches. The two scrambled around the ground for a moment. Somehow the Sorcerer seemed unable to use her magic. Given more time, the Mercenary might have pondered this, but not now. The thrill of violence was coursing through her veins. She was unstoppable!

Weakly, the Sorcerer shoved her rival with both feet. The Mercenary allowed herself to be dislodged and, with a smirk, she stood. This was far easier than she had expected; with all the pride and rage of a dragon, she reached down to draw her sword. Her hand clasped air.

'Missing something?'

The Mercenary growled and lunged again.

. . .

Windera had caught her toy. It had tried to run but now she had it. It was squealing and thrashing. It was funny.

'Get off me you mean little midget! Be gone you terrible beasty hairy thing. I've not done a thing to harm you let me go!' The toy blabbed. Windera found that the more she dug her talons in, the more she snapped her fangs near the toys throat, the more noise it made. It was fun.

The toy rolled suddenly to the side, its long limbs flailing. Windera dodged and giggled demonically; the toy looked somewhere between terrified and confused. Then it was off, running back towards the pretty pot that her mistress had made. Windera followed. Chasing games were fun.

'Look! Your mistress is in danger. Go help her!' The toy pointed a long finger towards Windera's mistress. She looked like she was having fun too. Windera shrugged and leaped at the toy. It fell to the ground wailing. Windera was having fun.

. . .

'You stole my sword!' The Mercenary screamed, flinging her cloak away and discarding the empty scabbard. If she was to win now she would need a little more mobility.

'Oh no, not me. Windera.'

'But you have magic!'

'I warned you it wasn't going to be a fair fight.' Mused the witch, swinging her fist towards the Mercenary's face

The Mercenary managed to block the punch, just barely, and clocked the Sorcerer in the jaw. The Sorcerer staggered to the side, grasping her face. Her victory did not last long. With a vengeance, the Sorcerer whirled back around, whacking the Mercenary with such force that she was flung to the ground.

'You know Mercenary, I could squish you like a bug. But this is too much fun. I have another two days to save Jadella, you have three minutes. Two fifty-nine, two fifty-eight...'

Spitting blood, the Mercenary staggered to her feet. She glared at her rival, calculating the distance between them. If not for that mongrel Windera she would have ended this fight in seconds; The Mercenary with No Name was a master swordsman, but a pathetic fist-fighter.

In the moments it took to think this, the Sorcerer had bounded up to one of the dunes. Her dress billowed around her, stained with dirt from her fall. It was so near to her feet; if the Mercenary could get her on the right angled slope she could probably make her trip...

Furiously, the Mercenary raced after her. She locked fists with the Sorcerer for a moment before spinning around and elbowing her in the ribs. The Sorcerer grinned. She was enjoying this. The Sorcerer aimed a high kick at the Mercenary, but slipped slightly on the loose sand; the Mercenary took advantage, catching her leg and spinning her around. The Sorcerer teetered, but still did not fall.

'Come on Mercenary, you're meant to be good at this sort of thing.' She taunted.

'It's been a long day.' The Mercenary grunted and stalked toward her rival, rage bubbling up inside her. This was taking too long. The third sun's glow was already bathing the horizon.

'I'm sure it has. And it is going to be your last!' Once more she charged, spinning and kicking, forcing the Mercenary to switch places. They both landed several blows, but none powerful enough to cripple the other. Still the Sorcerer refused to use her magic.

Then suddenly an opportunity arose. The Sorcerer was backed between a tuft of grass and a steep slope in the dune. Her left heel hung just over the bottom of her cloak. With one final grunt, the Mercenary shoved the Sorcerer backwards. She teetered dangerously, stepping back to steady herself - She stepped on her cloak. The Mercenary swelled with victory as her foe tumbled uncontrollably backwards – half into the grass, half exposed on the sand. Not wasting a moment, she pulled a stick from the undergrowth and approached the witch.

Suddenly realising her predicament, the Sorcerer raised a hand. She used her magic to tighten the skin around the Mercenary's throat, choking her. Mentally cursing, the Mercenary coughed, clawing at her neck. For a second the Sorcerer smiled. Then the Mercenary lurched forward, stick outstretched.

. . .

All of a sudden Windera stood erect. She allowed her toy to roll out from under her, still panting and making funny little terror noises. Windera did not laugh. There was something wrong. Something was gone. Like a phoenix out of water, she screeched off into the scrub. Her mistress. Her mistress. Something was wrong.

. . .

With a satisfying squelch, the stick was plucked from pale flesh. It was like a cork from a champagne bottle – gore spewed up from the hole in the Sorcerer's neck. The woman gurgled, blood dripping from her slack mouth. Her eyes rolled back in their sockets.

The Mercenary stood for a moment, then with grim satisfaction, spat on the Sorcerer and ran off down the dunes.

She skidded to a stop at the potion – which was now bubbling and smoking – and scooped it up. The third sun could be seen on the horizon. She had only seconds.

Thankfully, Jadella's hovel was just over the nearest sand dune. The Mercenary quickly bounded up and over, coming to an unsteady stop at the corpse of Jadella's maid; the wrench had begun to smell. She stepped over the body and knelt next to the powerful woman. She was in the same position as the day before – so peaceful. It was disgusting.

Hands shaking, the Mercenary poured the liquid into Jadella's slack mouth. Much of it missed – dribbling instead down her cheeks and onto her chest – but enough went in. Hopefully. Now all she could do was wait.

'Oh my bursting bubbles! Jadella's dead! You killed her. Oh no no no. Why would you do that?'

The Mercenary did not bother looking up. 'I was hoping you'd been killed. Relax, she'll be fine. She just needs the cure.'

'But... no, you can't cure a knife stab.' Nessaria blurted, her voice high and anxious, 'You just can't. Not with a potion anyhow. You killed her didn't you!'

The Mercenary glanced up at Nessaria irritably; she was fiddling nervously, looking as though she wanted to either help or run. The Mercenary with No Name prayed she would do the latter 'What are you babbling on about? Jadella poisoned herself.'

'With a knife?!You can't poison yourself with a knife. She was my friend you know. I provided her safe harbor three years running. Why else would I help you? And now this.'

Slamming the pot on the ground, the Mercenary growled, 'What are you talking about? This is Jadella!' She waved her hands at the woman still sleeping beside her.

'No it's not.'

The Mercenary faltered, 'What?'

'That's Jadella!' Nessaria wailed, flinging her long arms towards the corpse at the entrance to the hovel. 'The one you killed! Killed to death! Why would you do that? I thought you were a good person.'

The Mercenary felt her face go pale. Her mind flashed back to the moments before she killed the maid. She had whispered something; the Mercenary had thought nothing of it at the time. But if what she whispered was a spell then... then that meant... 'I...' The Mercenary stumbled forward. Sunlight was beginning to shine through the forest canopy.

Nessaria still kept her distance, but her banter had turned from that of grief to that of outrage, 'What? What do you have to say for yourself? You are a terrible, cruel, cheese-brain of a person with no morals and no conscience.' 'You deserve to rot in a pit you blasted blowfish. You-'

The Mercenary with No Name coughed and gasped; she felt suddenly feint, yet her head was throbbing. She used the last of her energy to look up one last time at the sun-bathed silhouette. 'Oh would you just shut up!' Then her arms gave way and she collapsed face first in the dirt.

57

Nessaria stared at her companion angrily for a moment; then a gasp yanked her attention towards the helpless figure of her friend, and until recently, Jadella's maid. Her eyes were open.

Chapter 11

jadella lies

Three golden suns blazed overhead, floating like candles in a foamy sea. Several trees bowed their leafy heads in sorrow, others stood rigid and skeletal like reapers. Even the birds had silenced.

'Tell me again what happened. How did you end up asleep in Jadella's place?' The Elf was so quiet; her voice smothered by the still air that lay over them like a cloak.

Her companion pulled her eyes from the stick-covered grave before them. Her eyes were puffy, but dry. 'We heard a rumour. The Mercenary with No Name, he... she was coming for us.' The Elf gently twirled her friend's hair affectionately. Her fingers got caught in a knot, and she began to tug. 'We thought- we thought that if she believed Jadella was trapped in a sleeping curse, then she would be off her guard and Jadella could kill her. Then she would wake me up and all would be well.'

Abandoning her attempt to untangle her fingers, the Elf let them hang in the Maid's hair, 'But the Mercenary killed her instead. How does something like that even happen? It's not like-'

'I think she wanted to die.' Her voice rang out over the sand dunes, 'I think she was sick of hiding, running, in fear of her very self. She probably cast a spell to wake me upon the Mercenary's death. It didn't matter that the Sorcerer had given her a poison. She knew I would be safe.' She looked up at the grave once more, 'And now she is too.'

After a moment, the Maid returned her gaze to her friend. She was uncharacteristically silent, and was clearly suffering from it, 'And what about you, old friend? How did you know to come here?'

Relieved, Nessaria jerked her finger from the Maid's hair, 'Oh that's a long story. Well, not too long, but you know. I came upon the Mercenary on a track, she was looking for a cure for 'the Great Jadella of Legend!' and I thought hmmm, this isn't quite right. So I tricked her, wriggled my way into her circle of trust and forced her to bring me along. I knew you were in trouble, see, and I knew you'd need me...

. . .

Windera snuffled around the grass. The effort of dragging her master left an ache in her muscles. Her claws had shredded her master's clothes and skin in places. But they did not bleed.

Once more, Windera placed a hand on her master's stomach. It did not rise nor fall. No pulse graced her furry fingers, no blood rushed through the stiff and shrunken veins. What had happened?

A sorrow-filled murmur escaped her crusted lips and she flopped back on her haunches. Her wings twitched, eager to be set loose to ride the winds. She wanted to leave. She did not want to see her master like this. She had to stay.

Suddenly a small voice whispered in Windera's head, growing louder and stronger with every word, 'And so the third sun has reached its rise, the fearless Mercenary has claimed her prize. And though she won, still she dies. Such is the price when Jadella lies…'

Her mistress's eyes snapped open.

ABOUT THE AUTHOR

Sonja Howard is 16 years of age. She lives where the rainforest meets the sea in Far North Queensland, Australia.
Sonja is known to many as Sonsational Creations and is an inspirational young Author and Artist.
Sonja's imagination continues to give life to many stories, works of art and mythical creatures.

To see more of her work please go to:
www.sonsationalcreations.deviantart.com
or
www.sonsationalcreations.etsy.com

www.ingramcontent.com/pod-product-compliance
Lightning Source LLC
Chambersburg PA
CBHW031901170626
46807CB00004B/1839